Oakleaf Academy

A Mystery at Fairy School

Melody Lockhart and Roberta Tedeschi

This edition published in 2023 by Arcturus Publishing Limited
26/27 Bickels Yard, 151–153 Bermondsey Street,
London SE1 3HA

Author: Melody Lockhart
Illustrator: Roberta Tedeschi
Story Editor: Gemma Barder
Project Editors: Claire Baker and Joe Harris
Designer: Rosie Bellwood

CH010414NT
Supplier 10, Date 0623, PI 00004906

Printed in the UK

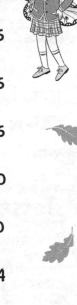

Meet the Oakleaf Girls!

Ivy

Ivy is a fairy ... but she's a bit of a rebel! She's dyed her pink hair black and she's not afraid to challenge traditional fairy ways and do things differently. She has an Ariel spark, which means she can do sky magic.

Jessamy

Jessamy's endlessly curious, and she never stops talking! This red-headed sprite gets really excited about everything—especially her Leafkin spark, which gives her forest magic.

Azalea

Azalea's a smart and stylish pixie. She tries to play it cool, but she can't hide how much she cares about her friends! Her snooty parents didn't like it when she got a Fishscale spark—but she's slowly learning to love her water magic.

Poppy

Poppy the brownie is small even compared to her friends, but she has a big heart. She grew up in a gallumpher's house—"gallumpher" is

what smallfolk like fairies, pixies, and sprites call us humans. Poppy's wand has an unusual, heart-shaped spark.

Chapter 1

A Package for Ivy

"So Ivy," huffed Azalea, "Tell me again exactly *why* I'm standing here getting honey on my brand-new shoes ... and all before breakfast?"

Ivy, Poppy, and Jessamy couldn't help but giggle at Azalea's sour face. She really wasn't a morning person.

It was the first day of the friends' second semester at Oakleaf Academy, and they were in the bee-mail room, where the students' letters and packages were left by friendly insects.

"I'm expecting a really cool package," said Ivy, who had woken up full of excitement and begged her roommates to come with her to pick it up. She was looking for her hexagonal shelf on the wall. "I can't wait to show you all!"

Poppy fluttered to her own hexagon and smiled as she pulled out a letter. Azalea found a postcard, and Jessamy pulled a small package from her shelf.

Ivy fluttered back from her hexagon, empty-handed. "I don't understand, it was supposed to be here ..." Just then, a particularly ancient bumblebee swooped in through the door.

It sighed with relief as it dropped its package at Ivy's feet. "Yes! At last!" she squealed.

Azalea said that she was literally *dying* for her morning cup of tree sap tea ... so the friends decided to open their bee-mails in the cafeteria. They knew that Azalea found mornings extra difficult, since pixies usually slept in the daytime.

"Ooh, my big brother's sent me a sundial watch!" said Jessamy, putting it on. "Isn't it super pretty? And the green matches my Leafkin spark!"

"It's perfect," said Poppy, looking up from her letter and smiling.

"And who's your letter from, Pops? Your uncle and aunt?"

"My dad," said Poppy, "He has *sooo* many questions about magic. It will take me all year to write the reply!"

When she had arrived at Oakleaf, Poppy hadn't understood how magic worked, either. She and her friends had been given special challenges to discover their magical talents—and Poppy had watched in amazement as the tips of their wands blossomed with glowing symbols. A star for sky-loving Ariels, a shell for watery Fishscales, a flower for wild Leafkins, and a jewel for rocky Groundlings.

"Good luck explaining *your* spark, Poppy ..." said Azalea, laughing. There was no chance of that. Not even the teachers understood the strange, heart-shaped spark on Poppy's wand.

Azalea tossed her postcard onto the table. "Mine's from cousin Tulip," she sighed. "She wants to tell me how *sorry* she is about my terrible news. Ugh. It's a Fishscale spark, not a deadly illness!"

Poppy gave Azalea's shoulder a gentle squeeze. Everyone else in Azalea's snooty family was an Ariel.

"My turn!" said Ivy, "Who wants to see what's in *my* package?"

She tore off the brown paper to reveal a guitar made of half a peanut shell, with fine spiderweb strings. "I can't believe it's finally here!" Ivy said, running her fingers gently along the shimmering strings. "It's just like Interstella's!"

"Who's Interstella?" asked Poppy.

Ivy's eyes widened. "Only the lead singer from the most amazing band *ever*—Interstella and the Comets! Surely you've heard of them!"

"Sorry," said Poppy, shaking her head. "I grew up in a gallumpher house ..."

"Yeah, you can't help that." said Ivy. "When *I* was growing up, my sister Holly and I used to spend hours listening to Interstella in our bedroom," said Ivy. "Of course, that was before Holly decided to start acting like a 'proper' fairy. Now she cares more about what people think of

her than she does about having fun."

Poppy saw that Ivy's face had fallen a little, so she changed the subject. "Hey, why don't you play something for us?"

Ivy immediately cheered up. She stood up and looped the guitar strap over her shoulder—but when she strummed the spiderweb strings, no sound came out.

"Well, that was ... very impressive," snorted Azalea.

"Could this help?" Jessamy said, fluttering over with a small, glowing rock in her palm. "It was still inside the packing paper."

"Of course!" Ivy took the dark orange stone and slotted it neatly into the bottom of the guitar. "Amber is what makes these guitars really sing. Now you'll see why Interstella and the Comets once played so hard that an old oak tree dropped all its acorns!" Ivy took a few steps backward, closed her eyes, raised her arm, and strummed the guitar strings like a true rock star. This time, the sound was loud. VERY loud. So loud that a fairy a few years older gasped with shock and dropped her breakfast tray ... sending berries rolling all over the floor.

At the sound of the clattering tray, Ivy's eyes shot open. The girl who had dropped the berries was Bluebell, her sister Holly's best friend. She was crouching

on the floor, picking up dirty, squashed food. She didn't look happy ...

"Bluebell!" Ivy said, taking off her guitar and rushing to help. "I'm so sorry!" As Poppy and Jessamy fluttered around the older fairy collecting the breakfast berries that had rolled away, Ivy spotted someone striding across the room. It was her sister, Holly.

"Ivy, what in Fairyland do you think you are doing?" cried Holly, her hands on her hips. For sisters, they looked very different. Holly's hair was long, pink, and shiny—whereas Ivy had dyed her short hair black. Holly wore neat little shoes, while Ivy wore heavy boots.

"It was an accident," muttered Ivy. "I was just testing out my new guitar."

Holly glanced at the guitar on the table in front of Azalea.

14

"Honestly, Ivy," Holly said crossly. "When are you going to stop messing around and start acting more fairylike?" But before Ivy could answer, Holly had fluttered away with Bluebell.

When a tinkling bell rang across the cafeteria, Ivy sighed and picked up her new guitar.

"Time for our first spark lessons! How exciting!" said Jessamy, getting ready to flutter off to the forest. "I can't wait to find out more about my Leafkin magic.

See you all at lunch!"

"I guess I should get my Fishscale lesson over with, then," said Azalea, spraying herself with lavender perfume.

"What's with the horrible scent?" asked Ivy.

"Well, would *you* want to smell like a stinky pond? Actually, don't answer that."

"I'm sure you'll survive," giggled Poppy. "Come on, Ivy—I'll walk with you. You need to drop off the guitar in our dorm room before class, right?"

"I guess so," said Ivy. As the two friends left the cafeteria, Ivy asked, "Where's your spark magic lesson, Poppy?"

"In the library," replied Poppy, "I'm having private lessons with Ms. Glimmer until the teachers figure out what to do with me. Apparently, she's found some crumbly old leaf scrolls that mention

'hearte sparkes.' What about you?"

"Mine is in the observatory. I just hope I don't bump into Holly on the way ..."

Poppy was determined to cheer up her friend. "You know, I would love to hear an Interstella and the Comets song. Could you sing one for me?"

Ivy grinned, took a deep breath, and began singing at the top of her voice.

"Ivy!" called a loud voice. The principal was fluttering down the hallway toward them. Uh-oh!

Chapter 2

Sugarplum Day

"I'm sorry, Ms. Peaseblossom!" Ivy said to the principal. "I was just ..."

"It's my fault, Ms. Peaseblossom," said Poppy, quickly. "I asked Ivy to sing for me, so she ..."

Ms. Peaseblossom held up her hands to silence them both, then swooped down to the ground. "My dears, everything is perfectly splendid. You're not in trouble. It was just a wonderful surprise to hear such a tuneful voice."

Poppy and Ivy sighed with relief.

"In fact, I think I have a blossomingly brilliant idea!" said Ms. Peaseblossom, fluttering off the ground again. "You simply must take part in the Sugarplum

Day performance, Ivy! Your sister Holly has already signed up."

"I don't think ... I mean, I can't ..." Ivy said, her eyes wide as she desperately tried to think of an excuse.

"What's the matter, dear?" asked Ms. Peaseblossom. "Don't you want to help your fellow fairies show the rest of the school what Sugarplum Day is all about?"

"Of course, I do," said Ivy with the best smile she could manage.

But Poppy knew Ivy too well. She could see that her friend didn't mean it.

"Wonderful!" said Ms. Peaseblossom, "Rehearsals start this evening in the grand hall. I'll see you there! Right, now I need to collect some more stardust before this morning's lesson." Then, she fluttered off around the corner.

"What's so bad about Sugarplum Day?" Poppy asked Ivy as they began to walk. "I thought it was a lovely celebration for fairies?"

Ivy sighed. "It is, but it's celebrating the worst fairy of all. Perfect Princess Sugarplum was the 'sweetest, prettiest princess that ever lived,'" Ivy said, sticking out her tongue in disgust. "All fairies get told the story of how one day she was snatched up by an evil dragon toad and carried away to the King of the

Boggarts. Of course, Princess Sugarplum was too fairylike—or useless, if you ask me—to even try to escape. She just waited to be rescued by a brave sprite warrior named Prince Noble. Noble defeated the dragon toad and the Boggart King, and the boggarts have been banished from being anywhere near fairies ever since."

"Oh, I see," said Poppy. "Is that why

boggarts are so shy? My dad says that they only come out when they're sure no one is around."

Ivy shrugged. "I guess so. I've never seen one. But what I *do* know is that every year, fairies everywhere are supposed to celebrate Princess Lazy-Plum for being *rescued* by a prince."

Poppy giggled at the face Ivy was pulling, but her expression changed as they reached the library. "Okay, I guess I should go in," she said nervously.

"You're going to be amazing," said Ivy. "I bet your dad was so proud when you told him about your spark."

Poppy glanced down at her wand, tucked neatly into her belt. "I think so," she began. "He spilled his tree sap tea when I first told him—but then he gave me a big hug. We didn't really talk about it for the rest of the vacation. I think he's a bit worried about it." Poppy sighed. "Actually, I'm a little worried, too. A one-of-a-kind spark seems like such a big responsibility. And like Azalea keeps saying, I've still got so much to learn about smallfolk—without trying to understand my spark, too."

Ivy grinned at her friend. "Yes, but unlike Azalea, you don't think you already know it all!"

Poppy laughed, then the two friends

said goodbye as Ivy headed off to the observatory.

As she fluttered along, Ivy felt much better about her bad start to the day. In fact, she thought, she always felt better after spending time with Poppy. It was no wonder she had been given a Heart spark—Poppy was such a caring friend!

Ivy pushed open the heavy doors of the observatory. Sunlight streamed onto the benches below the high glass dome, which were almost full with students. Ivy spotted a spare seat next to a leprechaun and fluttered toward it. "Is anyone sitting here?" Ivy asked the girl.

"No, please sit there, that seat's free.

Nice to meet you—I'm Sweetpea!"

Ivy smiled—she loved the way that leprechauns spoke in rhyme. "Hey Sweetpea, I'm Ivy. I think I saw you at the

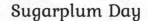

Ariel test last semester—you're amazing
at catching stardust!" Sweetpea smiled.

"You're right—I am good with a net.
But you have talents, too, I bet!"

Just then, Ms. Peaseblossom fluttered
into the observatory, her arms full of jars
filled with stardust.

Chapter 3

Music of the Stars

"Welcome, welcome, my astounding Ariel students," Ms. Peaseblossom began. "Last semester, you proved how wonderful you all are at catching stardust—one of the most magical substances in the world. And now you will learn how to make stardust dazzle, dance, and delight!"

Ms. Peaseblossom began to pop open the bottles of stardust. As she pulled out each cork, the stardust shot into the air and twirled around, leaving glittering trails behind it. The students made "Ooh!" and

26

"Aah!" sounds. It was like being at a fireworks show.

"But there's more to the night sky than stars!" said Ms. Peaseblossom. "And it's not just stardust that you need to learn about, but also ..." and here she paused for effect, "... moondust. Because these two magical substances are so different, your lessons will be split between two teachers—me and the magnificent Ms. Marigold."

Ivy was listening so hard to everything that Ms. Peaseblossom was saying, she almost didn't hear Sweetpea whispering in her ear:

"There's a secret that I know,
I heard it just a day ago.
Our magic teachers, this is true,
I've been told they're *sisters*, too."

Ms. Peaseblossom flashed Sweetpea a

stern look, and she stopped talking.

"During your Ariel test," the principal continued, "we challenged you to capture as much stardust as you could. But expert Ariels don't chase after stardust and moondust—they *dance* with them. And to do that, you must learn to hear their secret music."

Ivy thought of her guitar. If Ariel magic was all about music, that would explain why she'd been given the spark! She couldn't help but smile.

"Now, my Ariel acrobats," said Ms. Peaseblossom, fluttering back to the benches where the students sat. "It takes practice to be able to hear the music of the night sky—and that practice starts today. So come on, up you get!"

Ivy and Sweetpea grinned at each other and Sweetpea said:

"I may lack wings to fly up high,
But watch me *bounce* into the sky!"

Then, Sweetpea bent her knees and pushed herself high into the air.

It wasn't long before Ivy was swooping and swirling through the stardust. She remembered how wonderful it had felt during her Ariel test last semester, as though she was exactly where she was meant to be. She'd found it so effortless to catch stardust, too!

This time, though, things weren't proving quite so easy. As much as Ivy loved swooping through the stardust, she soon realized that she couldn't hear any music at all. As a smart-looking pixie swooped past her gently humming

a tune, Ms. Peaseblossom appeared, too, clapping her hands. "Good going, young Dandelion!" she said, fluttering next to the pixie. "You can hear it!" The pixie looked delighted with himself as he drifted off, still humming the tune.

Ivy's heart began to beat a little faster as more and more students started joining in with the music of the stardust. They sounded like a strange, humming choir. She flew alongside one stardust trail and listened really hard, but she couldn't hear anything. The next trail was silent, too. As hard as she tried, Ivy just couldn't hear one note.

"Now, those of you who can hear the music of the stars, see if you can change the tune a little," Ms. Peaseblossom said. She began to hum along to a silvery trail of stardust. "You can make the stardust

do things like change shape or even glow brighter."

Ivy watched as Sweetpea sprang into the air in a star jump. Instantly, a swirl of stardust beside her formed itself into the same star shape. Soon afterward, Dandelion found a way of humming that made a stardust swirl glow in five different shades of purple.

Then, Ms. Peaseblossom announced

that the class was over and asked the students to guide their stardust back into the jars. Ivy was the last student to return to the benches, squeezing every last moment out of the lesson before she gave up trying to hear the music.

Sweetpea gave Ivy's arm a gentle little squeeze.

"Please don't worry, my new friend,
I know you'll get there in the end."

At lunchtime, Jessamy was telling her friends all about her Leafkin lesson.

"We learned how to give butterflies new spots! And at the next Leafkin lesson, we're going to learn about enchanting tree sap!" She only stopped talking once, to quickly chew a pumpkin seed.

"Fascinating," said Azalea, squeezing

water from her hair and not sounding fascinated at all. "At least you stayed dry. The Fishscale magic teacher, Mr. Pondweed, wanted us to make little ripples with our wands. But everyone kept splashing each other. The water in the underground lake beneath the school is—surprise!—*not* my top choice of shampoo."

"How was your first lesson, Poppy?" asked Jessamy.

Poppy smiled. "It wasn't too bad. Ms. Glimmer translated some leaf scrolls, and it was interesting to hear about other people with Heart sparks. I would have loved to do some actual magic, though!"

Poppy glanced over the table at Ivy, who hadn't said a word since she'd sat down with her lunch tray.

"It's okay, Ivy," said Azalea. "I won't get

upset if you talk about your Ariel lesson. I've decided to make Fishscale the latest must-have spark!"

Ivy sighed. "It was fine," she said, pushing her lunch around her plate.

"Just fine?" said Jessamy. "No midair collisions, no stardust slip-ups?"

"Nope, all fine," Ivy said, getting up. "Come on, we'll be late for our Enchanted Objects lesson." With that, she quickly left the table.

Chapter 4

The Shadow in the Window

Later that day, when lessons ended, Ivy fluttered to the grand hall to join the Sugarplum Day rehearsals, just like Ms. Peaseblossom had asked her.

At one end of the hall, a group of sprites, brownies, fairies, and gnomes were all working together to prepare for the show. Only fairies would take part in the special performance, but everyone else wanted to help them get ready.

"Hey Ivy!" called Olive, a gnome she had made friends with last semester.

"Where should we put these jewels?" asked Oakley, Olive's twin brother. The twins had been the first students in the year to discover their Groundling spark

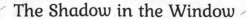

and were pushing a large wheelbarrow full of shiny green emeralds.

"Sorry," Ivy shrugged. "No idea!"

Ivy looked around the hall at the pretty pink decorations being hung in every corner to celebrate the story of Princess Sugarplum. She couldn't get excited about the bunches of pink flowers and fussy ribbon bows everywhere. But then, Ms. Peaseblossom had been nice about her singing voice, so she felt she should give Sugarplum Day a chance.

When Ivy spotted Holly and Bluebell standing in a group of fairies at the back of the hall, she took a deep breath, shook her wings, and headed toward them to say hello. Although she and Holly were so different now, Holly was still her big sister. Ivy wanted to make up with her.

"Hey Holly. Hey Bluebell," said Ivy, arriving next to her sister. "I just wanted

to say sorry again for making you drop your breakfast tray this morning. I really didn't mean to."

Bluebell smiled. "That's okay," she said. "The cafeteria staff ended up giving me an extra helping when I told them what had happened."

Holly looked at her sister. "I'm sorry if I was a little hard on you this morning," Holly said, and Ivy felt a warm glow inside her. She was always happier when she and Holly got along.

"So, are you going to play your guitar in the show?" asked Bluebell.

Before Ivy could reply, Holly laughed loudly. "I don't think so!" Holly said. "Sugarplum Day is all about Princess Sugarplum. The music should be sweet and pretty, just like her—not horrible, ear-splitting rock music!"

Ivy sighed. She remembered how Holly and she had sung along to rock music together in their bedroom. Those had been such happy times!

"You should play Princess Sugarplum in the show, Ivy," suggested Holly, clapping her hands and fluttering off the ground. "You've got such a nice voice—when you're not shouting out Interstella and the Comets songs, of course."

Suddenly, Ivy's warm glow cooled all the way down. Holly used to love Interstella and the Comets! "Actually, I think I'll just play in the orchestra or help out backstage," she said.

Holly tutted. "Oh, Ivy, seriously? Ms. Peaseblossom asked you to be in the performance. You can't let her down. Sugarplum Day is the most important day of the year for fairies."

"Not *this* fairy," snapped Ivy, angrily. "I don't want to wear a pretty dress and be saved by a prince. And I don't want to be fairylike either, thank you very much!"

"There's nothing wrong with being fairylike," replied Holly, coolly.

"You'll never understand," said Ivy, unhappily. Then, she whisked herself around and fluttered back out of the hall.

Ivy kept going until she'd flown straight

out of the Academy into the school grounds. She took deep breaths of the cool night air, hoping it would help her calm down. No one made Ivy as angry as Holly did—not even Azalea!

Ivy stared up at the twinkling stars. She closed her eyes and tried as hard as she could to hear their music. Perhaps the sound would be stronger out here? But all Ivy could hear were the faint sounds of the fairy orchestra preparing for Sugarplum Day.

Ivy opened her eyes again, feeling bitter with disappointment. But as she glanced toward the window of the school tower, she noticed the shadow of a person. They were moving around in a way that seemed somehow *sneaky*. Ivy fluttered up to take a closer look and was sure the shape wasn't a fairy or

a brownie, a sprite or a pixie, a gnome or a leprechaun. Ivy's heart beat faster. What were they? Should they be there? Just then, the shape turned toward the window—and let out a shriek! The figure jumped back with a clattering noise.

Ivy put her hand on the window and was relieved to find that it wasn't locked. As it swung open, she swooped inside.

Once inside, Ivy spotted the shadow quickly climbing a winding staircase that led to the library at the top of the tower. She caught a better glimpse of the creature as it passed a glowing mushroom light on the staircase wall. It was about the same size as Ivy, with green skin and a few strands of green hair on its bald head. It had large, pointed ears and wore a tattered tunic.

"Wait! Who are you?" Ivy shouted, bravely. But when the creature heard Ivy's voice, it ran off twice as fast, darting along the Academy's winding hallways. "Come back!" Ivy yelled, but she was losing sight of the creature. As she turned a corner into the hallway that led to the library, it was gone, as if it had simply vanished into thin air.

Ivy fluttered to the ground, out of breath. Whatever she'd seen definitely didn't want to be caught.

What type of creature was it? The way it had run away when it heard her voice told Ivy that whatever it was, it was more afraid of her than she was of it.

Chapter 5

The Book Thief

Ivy couldn't wait to tell her friends what had happened. But once she was back in the dorm room, she couldn't get the words out in the right order.

"Ivy, slow down!" said Poppy. Like Azalea and Jessamy, Poppy was already in her nightclothes, and Dazzle, their dorm pet glowworm, was ready for bed, too. "Now, start at the beginning—what *exactly* did you see?"

Ivy took a deep breath, shut the dorm room door, and sat cross-legged on the rug in front of Dazzle. "That's just it," she said. "I don't know who or what it was that I saw! All I know is that it didn't want to be caught snooping around Oakleaf

Academy. It was really sneaky."

"Ooh, what a mystery! What did it look like? Tell us everything!" said Jessamy, her bright-blue eyes wide with both excitement and wonder.

"It was green, mostly," replied Ivy. "It had green hair and green skin, and its clothes were sort of scruffy. It didn't look much older than us, though."

"Oooh! I bet it's the Ogre of Oakleaf!" Jessamy said, her wings trembling a little.

"The WHAT?" asked Poppy.

"The Ogre of Oakleaf! My brothers told me all about it. It looks for students who are out of bed, and it ... it ... well, they never get to the part where they tell me what it does, because they scare me so much I always fly away!"

Azalea sat up in her bed. "Oh, for goodness' sake, you're always telling us your brothers' silly stories, Jessamy," she said. "It definitely wasn't an ogre—they're bigger than gallumphers! What Ivy saw was a boggart."

Ivy was stunned. "A boggart?" she repeated. "But I thought that boggarts are really big and scary-looking?

48

Anyway, you never really see boggarts—not since they were banished."

Azalea tutted. "Boggarts aren't around during the day when smallfolk like you are out and about," she said. "But pixies like me are nocturnal, remember. We sometimes see boggarts at nighttime."

"But then, why would it run away? Boggarts aren't afraid of anyone, especially fairies!" argued Ivy. "In fact, they *hate* fairies—that's why they kidnapped Princess Sugarplum."

"Ivy," said Azalea. "It was absolutely, definitely a boggart."

Ivy suddenly felt very nervous. If there was one fairy-hating creature running around, there could be more. "Okay," she said, "In that case, I think we should all split up and search for it."

Azalea sighed as she slipped on a rose

petal eye mask. "There's really no point. everyone knows boggarts are very good at hiding. You'll never find him now."

"It is very late," said Jessamy, fluttering onto her bunk.

Ivy turned to Poppy, her eyes full of frustration. "Let's go and look tomorrow," Poppy said, kindly. "We should probably all get some sleep now. Even poor Dazzle looks exhausted!"

Snorting sulkily, Ivy put on her nightclothes and got into bed, but she couldn't fall asleep. She kept thinking about the terrible day she'd had. Two arguments with her sister had left her drained, and her first Ariel lesson had been a disaster. And now it seemed that the school was being invaded by fairy-hating boggarts.

"That's right, well done!" said Ms. Peaseblossom, clapping her hands as Ivy's second Ariel lesson got underway. "Sweetpea, you've managed to turn your stardust into a perfect, glowing orb!"

Sweetpea bounced happily back to her seat next to Ivy on the observatory benches, but Ivy couldn't stop thinking about the creature she'd seen the night before. Concentrate, she thought to herself. You'll never hear the music of the stars if you keep on like this.

"Ivy, dear!" called Ms. Peaseblossom, cheerfully. "Why don't you try it?"

Ivy took a deep breath and slowly walked to the front of the class, where Ms. Peaseblossom was making a whoosh of stardust spin in a circle around her.

"Now, Ivy, take a moment to really listen. Once you can hear the music, you can begin to shape the stardust." It sounded impossible to Ivy after her last lesson, but she was determined to try again—and she did love music, after all. Ivy closed her eyes. At first, she heard nothing but her fellow students shuffling in their seats. Then, slowly she heard a faint tinkling sound. Gradually, it got louder and louder until ... yes! At last! Ivy could hear the music!

Ivy was so excited. "I've done it!" Ivy said, fluttering her wings. "I can hear the music, I really can!"

With a wave of her hand, Ms. Peaseblossom guided the stardust toward Ivy. It settled just above her head.

"Wonderful!" said Ms. Peaseblossom. "Now, really concentrate, and try to shape the stardust the best you can."

Ivy began to hum and sway with the music, as it got louder and louder in her

ears. The stardust started to spin around, slowly at first—then faster and faster, until it was like a tiny tornado!

"Gently, Ivy, take your time," Ms. Peaseblossom said, a hint of warning in her usually calm and cheerful voice. "We don't want the stardust to get out of control ..."

Ivy's eyes widened. The stardust was twisting and turning and glowing brighter and brighter until ...

BOOM!

Smoke filled the observatory. Instead of music, all Ivy could hear now was everyone coughing and spluttering. Ms. Peaseblossom whizzed around the room opening all the windows. "Not to worry!" she said brightly. "These things can happen when we're learning to control the power of stardust. I think perhaps we should leave it there for the day, though. Class dismissed!"

Ivy didn't move. She couldn't believe she'd just made stardust explode in front of the whole class! Ms. Peaseblossom fluttered closer. "Don't worry, Ivy, my dear," she said. "You obviously have plenty of power to use—and it's my job to teach you the way to control it."

"Thank you," said Ivy, then added, "Ms. Peaseblossom, have you ever seen a boggart in the school?"

"Oh, goodness me!" Ms. Peaseblossom giggled. "Have Jessamy's big brothers been telling her stories again? Boggarts wouldn't dare come near the school." Ms. Peaseblossom's face grew serious. "But Ivy, if you do ever see a boggart, please stay as far away as possible. Boggarts don't like us fairies at all, and it would be very dangerous for you to meet one, however unlikely."

Ivy nodded as she hurried off.

As much as she hated the idea of Sugarplum Day, Ivy knew she couldn't miss the next rehearsal. She'd promised Ms. Peaseblossom, and she didn't want Holly to be angry with her either. That was why she was now learning a dance that meant she had to be on her tiptoes—a little tricky in her chunky boots!

As soon as Ivy could slip out for a break, she headed to the hallway where she'd seen the strange creature the night before. Creeping along the long hallway that led to the library, she tried not to make a sound.

Then, suddenly, she gasped! There was the creature again, hiding behind a doorway and panting as though it were very out of breath! Now Ivy was sure Azalea had been right after all. It was definitely a boggart—it looked just like the drawings Ivy had seen in every Princess Sugarplum storybook, although smaller and not covered in boils.

When the boggart spotted Ivy, its eyes were wide with terror. It ran away as fast as its little green legs could carry it!

This time, Ivy didn't chase after it. Instead, she stepped into the library. Inside, there was a terrible mess. Books has been pulled down from the shelves and thrown on the floor. Did the boggart do this? she wondered. Perhaps it had been looking for something ...

"What happened?" Ivy asked the friendly bookworms who looked after the library. The bookworms couldn't talk, but they wanted to help. They guided Ivy to a dusty corner of the library that was full of old, dried-up leaf scrolls. Then, the bookworm at the front of the line bent his long body toward a scruffy-looking scroll that had been unrolled and left lying on the floor.

"It's a map," Ivy said, picking it up gently. "And it looks like it's of the school. "But all the writing looks like it's in a different language." The bookworms nodded, then shuffled off to tidy up, leaving Ivy more confused than ever!

Chapter 6

Interstella

"So, what you're saying is ... I was right?" Azalea said at breakfast the next morning, smiling smugly.

"Yes, okay, you were right, it was a boggart," said Ivy, rolling her eyes. "But that's not the point. The point is, I think he was looking for this!"

Ivy unrolled the map and placed it on the table for her friends to see. "But what does it all mean?" asked Poppy.

"I don't know," admitted Ivy. "If only we could read all this writing, that would be a start."

Jessamy squealed. "Oooh, I know what that is!" she said. "It's ancient Sprite!" Poppy, Ivy, and Azalea stared at her in confusion. "We sprites get taught a little ancient Sprite—the old language—when we're young. I think I can translate it, but it might take awhile."

"But what about the boggart?" asked Poppy. "Weren't you afraid of it, Ivy?"

Ivy thought for a moment. "Actually, no, not really," she said. "In fact, he looked much more frightened of me than I was of him—and he ran away before I could get very close."

Just then, Holly appeared at the friends' breakfast table, and Ivy quickly rolled the scroll back up. "Hey Hols," Ivy said, trying to act as normal as possible. She didn't want her sister to know that she'd been chasing a boggart around the school halls instead of rehearsing for the Sugarplum Day show. Ivy suspected that Holly would send a bee-mail to their parents right away.

"Hey Hols? Is that all you've got to say?" Holly asked. "After you sneaked

out of Sugarplum Day rehearsals early two days in a row! The only reason Ms. Peaseblossom doesn't know is because Bluebell and I have covered for you."

"I'm really sorry," Ivy began. "But there's a very good reason, I promise."

"I'd love to hear it ..." Holly said, raising her eyebrows.

Ivy looked at her friends. Poppy smiled in encouragement, but Ivy shook her head. "I'm sorry Holly, I can't tell you. Not right now. But it's important, it really, honestly is."

Holly threw her hands up and fluttered into the air. "You've got one last chance, Ivy," she said. "Make sure you come to rehearsals on Saturday, or I'll have to tell Ms. Peaseblossom!"

Then, Holly turned away and flew off to her first lesson of the day.

Ivy took a deep breath before she went into the observatory for her final Ariel lesson of the week. She felt like such a failure! She'd struggled to hear the soft tinkling music the stardust made ... then she'd got so carried away that she had caused an explosion!

Ivy sat down on a bench next to Sweetpea, then noticed that Ms. Peasebossom was missing. Instead, there was a tall fairy with short purple hair at the front of the class. She was wearing stylish clothes and a long cape, and the most amazing necklaces Ivy had ever seen. She looked familiar, although Ivy couldn't think where she might have seen her before.

"Who's that?" whispered Ivy.

"Our teacher's sister, we've been told—
It's time to meet Ms. Marigold."

"Well, now!" began Ms. Marigold, bending down to roll out two sturdy-looking barrels from under her desk. "It's good to meet you all. The way I hear it, Ms. Peaseblossom has been teaching you all about stardust—and some of you have been really feeling that groove. But now, we're going to shake things up! I'm going to teach you about moondust."

As Ms. Marigold pulled out the stoppers from both barrels, a bright-yellow light shot out. It didn't twirl and swoop like stardust, but bounced off the walls and ceiling, as though it were in a terrible hurry.

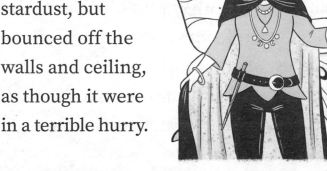

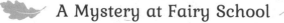

"Moondust!" Ms. Marigold continued, looking up at the observatory roof with her hands on her hips. "It's wilder and harder to control than stardust, but it works in much the same way. All you have to do is listen for the music."

Ivy's heart sank. It had taken her ages to tune in to stardust, and when she finally did, it had been a complete disaster. Now she was going to have to start all over again with moondust!

Ivy joined the other students as they flew and jumped through the sparkling dust, concentrating as hard as she had done when she first heard the music of the stars. But to her surprise, Ivy's ears were filled with loud, wild music almost right away— the best she had ever heard! She didn't recognize the instruments, but she loved the fast-paced beats and catchy tunes.

The moondust flew around her in happy bursts, but just as quickly as it had shot out of the barrels, it disappeared and the music faded away.

"That was amazing! But where did the moondust go?" Ivy asked Sweetpea breathlessly, as everyone sat down again.

"They say stardust lasts much longer,

But that moonlight is much stronger," Sweetpea replied.

At the end of the lesson, Ivy waited until everyone had left before she shyly

approached Ms. Marigold. The grown-up fairy smiled at her, taking in Ivy's jet-black hair and heavy boots.

"Can I help with something?" asked Ms. Marigold.

"Yes, it's just I couldn't really hear stardust at first," Ivy began. "But I was wondering why the moondust was so loud? It seemed to fill the whole room!"

Ms. Marigold laughed. "Wow! You sound just like me at your age. It's nothing to worry about, I promise. In fact, my kid sister could hear stardust way before I could."

Ivy sighed with relief, realizing how different Ms. Marigold was from her own sister, Ms. Peaseblossom. It was just like her and Holly!

"Thank you, Ms. Marigold," she said.

"Call me Stella, please! It's much less old and stuffy," Ms. Marigold replied.

Ivy blinked. "Stella?" she said, stunned. Suddenly, she knew why Ms. Marigold looked so familiar. "You're not Interstella, are you? From Interstella and the Comets?"

Ms. Marigold grinned. "I certainly am."

Chapter 7

In Search of the Boggart

Ivy couldn't wait to tell her friends that Ms. Marigold was actually a famous rock star. Her own teacher was actually Interstella! The *real* Interstella from Interstella and the Comets! But as soon as she entered the dorm room, Jessamy grabbed her by the shoulders and twirled her around.

"I've done it!" Jessamy said, excitedly. "I've actually done it!"

"Done what?" Ivy asked, once Jessamy finally let her go.

"The writing on the map, I've figured out what it says!"

Poppy rushed over with the map, and even Azalea looked up with interest from

the book she was reading. "It says that Princess Sugarplum's sword is hidden somewhere in the school grounds," explained Jessamy.

Azalea raised an eyebrow. "Princess Sugarplum never had a sword in the stories. It must mean Prince Noble's sword." said Azalea. "You fairies lost it just after Princess Sugarplum was rescued. A little careless, really, but at least we might be able to find it again, now."

Ivy couldn't help smiling, in spite of Azalea's snarky tone. She knew her friends were just as excited as she was by the map and its message.

"But wait," said Poppy. "If the boggart saw the map on the floor, won't he know where the sword is, too?"

"Probably," said Jessamy. "Ancient Sprite is very similar to ancient Boggart."

"Yikes," said Ivy, her voice cracking slightly. "Then, that means we have to stop him from finding the sword.

All fairies know how powerful Prince Noble's sword is. Its magic was used to defeat a dragon toad, and they're pretty much unbeatable! If the boggart finds the sword before we do, Sugarplum Day will be ruined!"

"Not just Sugarplum Day," said Azalea. "If a boggart was running around the school with a magical sword ... let's just say I wouldn't want to be a fairy."

Ivy shivered. She thought of Holly and Bluebell, of Ms. Marigold and Ms. Peaseblossom, and of all the other fairies at Oakleaf who might be in danger if the boggart found the sword.

"I'll follow the map tomorrow morning," she said, bravely. "Hopefully, I won't be too late."

"Don't you mean *we* won't be too late?" said Poppy, smiling. "You're not doing this on your own."

"Nope, we're all coming!" said Jessamy. "Aren't we, Azalea?"

"If you insist," Azalea drawled, waving her wand. "I suppose it could be a pretty interesting way to spend a Saturday. And besides," she continued with a small smile, "boggarts hate water, so my spark could come in handy. Any sign of trouble, and I'll magic up a steaming bubble bath full of relaxing lavender oil."

Ivy giggled—then shook her head. "It's too dangerous!" she said. "And what if you all get into trouble? Ms. Peaseblossom told me to stay away from any boggarts, and here I am chasing after one!"

Poppy and Jessamy huddled around Ivy. "We're friends, and friends help each other out," Poppy said.

Ivy felt a warm glow spread all through

her body, as though she'd just gulped down a whole cup of delicious hot spiced apple nectar.

"Thank you so much, all of you," Ivy said. "You've all helped so much since I found that old map."

"We'll leave first thing in the morning. I can't risk bumping into Holly, she'll drag me straight into Sugarplum Day rehearsals."

"Won't she be cross when she finds out you're not there—again?" asked Jessamy.

"Maybe," replied Ivy, staring down at the map. "But it's a risk that I'm willing to take."

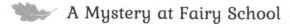

In the grounds of the Academy the next morning, Ivy, Poppy, Azalea, and Jessamy followed a bushy tail that bobbed up and down in front of them.

Before leaving the dorm room, the four friends had studied the map carefully. It hadn't taken them long to realize that the sword was hidden somewhere in the forest that lay to one side of the Academy.

They just needed to find a dark cave there, hidden by vines.

As soon as they had entered the forest, Jessamy had found a friendly squirrel to help guide them. She had used a twig to draw a rough copy of the map in the dirt, and the clever squirrel had seemed to quickly understand what they needed.

"Are you sure your squirrel friend knows where he's going?" asked Azalea.

"Of course!" said Jessamy. "This little guy's helped me before. He wouldn't do this if he didn't know the right way to go."

"How can you tell? All I heard was squeaking," said Azalea. "Are you sure he's not just leading us to his winter nut store?"

Jessamy giggled. "Fingers crossed!"

"I don't really understand how my magic works yet," said Poppy, "but I think it might have to do with feelings. And

I have a *good* feeling about Jessamy's squirrel friend here."

As they walked on, the forest grew darker and colder. Only a few rays of sunlight had managed to break through the thick canopy of leaves above their heads. Even Jessamy's chatter was starting to slow down. "We're a long way into the forest, aren't we?" she said.

"Yes, and who knows where we're stepping?" sighed Azalea. "My new shoes weren't made for hiking, you know."

"Aren't those the same ones that got covered in honey?" giggled Jessamy.

"We can't give up now," said Ivy. "We must be nearly there."

Poppy pulled out her wand again. The warm red glow from her spark was burning brighter than ever. "Yes, I think we must be getting close," she said.

Just then, the squirrel stopped at the base of a large, ancient-looking tree with sprawling, twisted roots covered in tangled vines. He twitched his whiskers and chittered. Then, with a flick of his bushy tail, he scampered off.

Jessamy watched until she couldn't see even the tiniest glimpse of red fur between the trees. "I suppose that means we're here—and we're all on our own!" she said, as cheerfully as she could.

"Now what?" asked Azalea.

"Now," said Ivy, lifting up the vines to reveal the entrance to a dark, shadowy cave. "We go inside ..."

With only the light of their wands to guide them, the four friends stepped nervously inside the dingy cave.

Right away, they heard a strange, muffled noise that echoed around the cave walls.

"Hmlmp!"

"What was that?!" hissed Azalea.

"Hmlmp!!" There was the noise again!

"I think it came from over here," said Poppy, using her wand to cast a bright glow.

As they got closer, the friends were dazzled by a huge pile of gold coins and shiny treasure. Bottles of stardust, stolen from the school, peeked out among the

numerous jewels—and on top sat a huge, slimy creature.

"Oh, no! That's ... a dragon toad!" whispered Ivy. "And all that shiny stuff must be its hoard."

"Hmmm, I think now would be a good time to run ..." said Azalea, stepping backward.

"I don't always agree with Azalea," said Ivy. "But this time, she's right. Dragon toads are dangerous. They are known for kidnapping smallfolk and stealing their treasure. We know Prince Noble's sword is here somewhere—if the dragon toad gives it to the boggart, he'll be a real danger to all the fairies at Oakleaf!"

"Wait a minute, though," said Poppy. "Look what the dragon toad is holding!"

The friends nervously peered closer. Now they could see exactly where the boggart was—held tightly in the dragon toad's slimy arms. "I told you! The boggart is already here!" said Ivy.

"Yes, but look at him. He's just a little thing," said Jessamy, "and he seems pretty frightened."

"Actually ... it looks like he's trying to get away," said Poppy, as she watched the boggart squirm and wriggle, his face crinkled with fear. "And something tells me he needs our help," she added. As she spoke, the heart at the tip of her wand glowed even brighter.

"I agree," said Azalea, bravely.

"Oh, yes—me, too!" said Jessamy.

They all looked at Ivy. "I trust you, Poppy," she said, squeezing Poppy's shoulder. "Let's rescue a boggart!"

Chapter 8

Trapped

Ivy wondered what Holly would say if she could see her right now—about to battle a dragon toad and rescue a boggart! She didn't have long to think about it, though, since the dragon toad hadn't taken long to spot the four smallfolk students. As the creature started to lumber toward them, piles of coins and jewels spilled across the cave.

The boggart had seen them, too. "Please help me!" he cried. He didn't sound at all monstrous or scary.

"Everybody split up!" called Ivy. She, Poppy, Jessamy, and Azalea ran in different directions.

Jessamy took out her wand.

Concentrating as hard as she could, she summoned a great gust of leaves that swirled around and around the dragon toad's head. The monster bellowed and rushed toward her.

Then it was Azalea's turn. She pointed the glowing seashell tip of her wand toward a puddle on the cave floor, and the murky water splashed up into the dragon toad's eyes. The monster shook its head in fury, turned around, and lurched toward her instead.

Poppy ran up behind the creature. "Leave that little boggart alone, you big bully!" she called, bopping the creature's tail with the tip of her wand. It began to slowly turn around.

Meanwhile, Ivy dashed forward to the bottles of stardust in

the heap of treasure. She wished it was moondust instead, but she didn't have any choice. She was just about to pop open her first bottle of stardust when she spotted something long, thin, and shiny peeking out from the treasure. A sword!

As Jessamy, Poppy, and Azalea took turns distracting the dragon toad, Ivy gently pulled out the sword. She'd seen Prince Noble's sword in picture books, and this one looked exactly the same— except for the handle, which was a bright shade of glittering pink. It was the exact same shade of pink, in fact, as Princess Sugarplum's hair in the books.

Ivy felt the heavy weight of the sword in her hand, but to her surprise, she had no trouble holding it. In fact, she felt a huge power surge from it through her body. Suddenly, it didn't matter that she was a tiny fairy—she really felt that there was nothing she couldn't do.

Ivy glanced back at her friends. She could see that Jessamy's magic was starting to run down, and the leaves were just gently rustling around the dragon toad's feet now. Azalea and Poppy looked exhausted, too.

Without a second thought, Ivy leapt in front of the toad and held the sword up high above her head. The dragon toad's eyes began to bulge. Its whole body shook with anger. It opened its slimy mouth and let out a deafening roar that made the cave tremble. Rocks began to fall from the cave roof.

But the dragon toad was so taken up with his anger at the little fairy, that he let go of the still struggling boggart. The small green creature picked himself up from the floor—but instead of running away as the friends expected, he started rummaging around in the treasure.

"Hey!" shouted Azalea angrily, over the dragon toad's roars. "Now is *not* the time to be filling your pockets!"

But the boggart had picked something up—a bottle of stardust! The friends watched, surprised, as he tossed it to Ivy.

"Here," he called, "Use your spark! Dragon toads may love twinkling treasures—but they *hate* bright lights!"

Then, he dived back into the treasure pile, jumping from bottle to bottle and pulling them open.

"How did you know about my spark?" Ivy asked, a little shocked that she was talking to a real-life boggart.

"There's a star on your wand, silly!" shouted the boggart.

Now that so many bottles had been uncorked, the whole cave was filled with silvery stardust trails. The huge dragon toad stopped roaring. It was staring at the dust with wide eyes and shifting around nervously.

Ivy dropped the sword, so that she could open the final bottle of stardust, letting it swoosh around the cave. She

closed her eyes tight and concentrated as hard as she could.

"You can do it!" said Poppy, squeezing Ivy's arm.

"Of course she can!" said Jessamy and Azalea, together.

Ivy began to hear the music of the stars. It tinkled around her head until she could feel each note from the tips of her fingers to her toes. It wasn't quite as strong as the music she'd heard from the moondust, but it was definitely there.

She imagined that Ms. Marigold was cheering her on, then that Princess Sugarplum was there, too. But Ivy didn't picture Princess Sugarplum in her pretty dress being rescued by a sprite prince. She imagined her holding the sword up high in the air as she flew back to her

castle, victorious at having defeated a dragon toad all by herself.

Suddenly, Ivy felt stronger and more powerful than she had ever felt before. She pulled out her wand and waved it in the air—and was delighted to see the stardust follow it like a magnet. Ivy took a deep breath and pointed her wand toward the dragon toad. The stardust followed it, covering the slimy creature and making him sparkle as if he were covered in thousands of tiny diamonds.

The glittering toad shone brighter and brighter, until the friends and the boggart had to shield their eyes against its glow. Then, just as the whole cave filled with light, Ivy, Poppy, Azalea, and Jessamy heard a small noise, a little like the pop of a soap bubble. As they nervously uncovered their eyes, they realized that the dragon toad had … disappeared.

All that remained were a few tiny sparkles, as trails of stardust melted into the air where the dragon toad had once been sitting.

"You did it!" said Poppy, throwing her arms around Ivy.

"I did, didn't I?" Ivy replied, giggling but sounding a little shocked.

Then, Jessamy and Azalea joined the hug, and the four friends jumped up and down for joy. The boggart started

jumping, too.

"Wait!" Azalea said eventually. "There are two things here that are slightly bothering me." She straightened her school tie and brushed some dirt off her blazer. "Number one, it seems like everything we thought we knew about boggarts is wrong."

"And number two?" asked Jessamy.

"That!" Azalea pointed to what had been the entrance to the cave. The dragon toad's almighty roar had shaken everything up, and now it was completely blocked with a mixture of mud, rocks, and sticks.

"Oh, no—that *is* a problem," said Jessamy, for once not sounding her usual cheery and upbeat self.

The friends were surprised to hear the boggart speak next. "P–perhaps I can help dig us out?" he said, a little nervously. For a moment, nobody replied, then Poppy stepped forward.

"Thank you, that's really kind," she said. "What's your name?"

"Pickerel," replied the boggart.

"I don't understand," said Ivy, still keeping her distance from the boggart. "Why would you help us? I thought boggarts *hated* fairies."

The boggart looked down. "That's what everyone thinks," he said. "But there was a time, long ago, when boggarts and other smallfolk lived together very happily."

Ivy's mouth dropped open.

"About a year ago," said Pickerel, "I found a fairy book about Princess Sugarplum. The story was completely different from the one I had been told when I was little! So I set out to uncover

the truth. I learned that there was a map in your school—a map that would lead me to that sword. And the sword can reveal the true story."

Then the boggart shuddered. "But when I got here, I saw that the dragon toad was guarding the sword—and he wasn't about to let it go! If you four hadn't turned up, I don't know what would have happened to me."

"But ... how can a sword tell you the truth about anything?" asked Poppy.

"Because Princess Sugarplum's sword is magical, of course," replied Pickerel patiently.

"You said 'Princess Sugarplum's sword.'" said Ivy, picking up the blade and staring at it. "Don't you mean *Prince Noble's* sword?"

Pickerel burst out laughing. "Prince Noble?" he spluttered. "I hardly think ..."

Just then, Pickerel was interrupted by a distant voice. It seemed to be coming from the other side of the cave entrance.

The four friends and the boggart quickly clambered over the mud and rocks. "Hello?!" said the slightly muffled voice from outside. "Is anyone in there?"

"Yes, we are!" cried Ivy.

"The entrance is blocked up!" called Poppy in her loudest voice.

"And it's really dirty in here!" grumbled Azalea under her breath.

"Ivy, are you all right?" called the voice.

Ivy fluttered off the ground. "I know that voice!" she said, happily. "Holly, is that you?"

Chapter 9

Sisters

On the other side of the cave entrance, Holly stood anxiously wondering how she was going to get her sister and her friends out.

Holly had known that something was wrong when Ivy hadn't turned up for that day's Sugarplum Day rehearsal. When Holly hadn't been able to find her sister or her roommates anywhere in the Academy, she'd been very worried. And when Ivy's classmates told Holly how they'd seen Ivy and her friends heading toward the forest, Holly hadn't wasted any time trying to find them.

Pulling out her gem-tipped wand, she'd used her earth-based Groundling

magic to search for footprints. When she had sensed rocks falling nearby, she had started running!

"I'm sorry, Holly," Ivy called through the blocked entrance. "I'll explain everything as soon as we get out of here, I promise!"

Holly shook her head. At first, she'd been both worried and angry, but now all that mattered was helping her little sister to safety.

"Never mind all that," Holly called. "We need to get you out of there! I can use my Groundling magic to move some of the rock and soil from the entrance. I'll need some help, though. Jessamy, are you in there? Could you summon some woodland animals to start digging?"

Jessamy looked at her wand nervously. "Um, we haven't been taught how to do that yet," she said. "That's next semester."

Ivy's eyes darted around the cave. "There were some bottles of stardust!" Ivy called to Holly. "We used it to get rid of the dragon toad, but there might be some left that we can use!"

"A dragon toad?!" Holly shouted back. "You got rid of what, Ivy?"

"I told you, I can explain everything—once we get out of here!"

The four friends began to rummage through the treasure, helped by Pickerel. They checked empty bottle after empty bottle, searching for one last drop of stardust. But there was none left. They'd used all of it in the cave to defeat the dragon toad.

"We'd better get out soon," said Azalea. "I mean ... I haven't even brought a change of clothes with me!"

Just then, Jessamy appeared from the back of the cave, clutching a bottle.

"I found some more stardust!" she said, excitedly.

"That's definitely not stardust," said Ivy, recognizing the silvery substance from her lesson with Ms. Marigold. "That's moondust!"

Together, the friends hurried to the cave entrance. "Holly!" Ivy called excitedly. "We've found a bottle of moondust!"

"Fantastic!" replied Holly. "Now, after I count to three, point the bottle at the entrance and take out the stopper. It should blast forward without anyone needing to use their wands."

"No, no!" said Ivy. "We should set the moondust free, then I'll guide it toward the entrance with my wand. I have a talent for moondust—Ms. Marigold said so. And by the way, Holly, do you know who Ms. Marigold really is?"

"I'm not sure that I care right now!" Holly snapped. "No, let's stick to my plan. I'm the oldest, and I know much more about magic than you do!"

"But I got the Ariel spark, not you!" Ivy snapped back.

Pickerel cleared his throat. "Excuse me," he said. "Could I make a suggestion?" Then, the boggart silently handed Princess Sugarplum's sword to Ivy.

"Who was that?" asked Holly, slightly shocked to hear a voice she knew didn't belong to Ivy or any of her friends.

"Oh, that's just Pickerel," called Jessamy cheerfully. "He's a boggart!"

"A boggart?!" Holly cried.

Ivy glared at Jessamy. She hadn't planned to tell Holly about the boggart just yet.

"Ivy! You need to get out of there right now!" Holly shouted.

"It's fine! The boggart's fine!" Ivy called, as she took the sword from Pickerel. "Like I said, I'll explain everything later!" Then, she looked from the sword to the boggart. "I don't understand," she said. "Should I use the sword to dig us out? Because that seems a bit silly when we all have wands and magic we can use."

Pickerel smiled. "It's like I told you! The sword is magic. Use it with the wand, and your magic will work even better. If your sister helps, we'll be free in no time!"

Ivy stared at Pickerel uncertainly. A week ago, she would never have believed she would be prepared to take advice from an actual real-life boggart!

"Now, Holly—you need to listen to me and do what I tell you," Ivy said, patiently. "On the count of three, use your Groundling spark magic to make the soil on your side move toward you. I'm going to use Princess Sugarplum's sword from this side of the entrance."

"Don't you mean Prince Noble's sword?" replied Holly, shocked. "Ivy, are you sure you haven't been put under a boggart spell? We all know Princess Sugarplum doesn't have a sword."

Ivy sighed. "Oh, yes, she does!" she called back. "And I've discovered there's a lot more to the Princess Sugarplum story that we've never been told!"

"I don't want to sound rude," said Azalea. "But would you two mind saving your catch-up until after we've escaped from this horrid hole under the tree?"

"Holly, are you ready?" Ivy called.

On the other side of the cave entrance, Holly hesitated for a moment, then raised her wand. "Ready!" she called. "On the

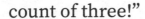

count of three!"

"I think we'd better get out of the way just in case," said Poppy. As she ushered Azalea and Jessamy to the back of the cave, her wand began to glow. Then, suddenly, a stream of warm red light flowed from the end of it, which spread out to make a protective dome around the three friends.

"Wow, Poppy!" Jessamy said, her eyes wide with wonder. "Did you know you

could do that?"

"Um, honestly, no," Poppy replied, huddling closer to her friends.

"One, two ..." Ivy and Holly shouted together.

Then, Pickerel pulled the stopper out of the bottle of moondust.

"... three!"

The moondust shot around the cave, filling Ivy's ears with music. Ivy held the sword in one hand and her wand

in the other. She concentrated as hard as she could on the music and drew the moondust toward her.

Then, as the moondust swirled forward, Ivy swung the shining blade of Princess Sugarplum's sword! She blasted the moondust into the pile of rocks that were blocking the cave entrance.

On the other side of the entrance, Holly held up her own wand and used her Groundling magic to move the rubble away. As the sisters worked their magic, the whole cave rumbled and shook. Pieces of mud and stone flew around the walls, bouncing off the protective dome that Poppy had put around her friends. From inside it, they watched Ivy nervously, but it seemed as though her magic kept anything from hitting her at all.

At last, the moondust fizzled away. Ivy dropped to the floor, exhausted, the sword still clutched in one hand.

"Ivy? Are you okay?" Ivy looked up to see Holly fluttering toward her.

Getting up again, Ivy gave her sister a twirling hug. "Thank goodness you're okay!" said Holly.

"I'm so sorry, Holly, I should have told you everything from the start," said Ivy, as they both hurried out of the cave.

As the protective dome drifted away from around them, Poppy, Azalea, and Jessamy left the cave, too. Pickerel stayed a few nervous steps behind them, but Ivy quickly fluttered over to him.

"Holly, meet Pickerel," she said. "Believe it or not, he's a boggart."

"But he's so small!" Holly said. "And where are his pointed teeth and boils?"

Pickerel laughed. "We boggarts never had boils," he said. "Or pointed teeth. Someone said we did many years ago, and all the smallfolk just believed it."

"Why would *anyone* make up a story like that?" asked Holly, astonished.

Chapter 10

New Sugarplum Day

In the library, the bookworms were patiently filling a table with old, crinkling leaf scrolls. When they'd finished, Pickerel began to unfurl them and lay them out in a special order. Then, he took Princess Sugarplum's sword from Ivy and laid it in the middle of the table.

"There," said Pickerel. "That should be everything we need."

Azalea peered over the boggart's shoulder. "That's very impressive," she said. "But we may need a little more information. I mean, all these scrolls are written in ancient Sprite."

"Oh, yes!" Jessamy said, fluttering high above them. "I'd love to translate them, but I think I'll be gone from the Academy for good before I get to the end of all those!"

Pickerel chuckled. "Don't worry, you won't need to do that," he said. "We just need someone with a Heart spark to show us what it all means."

Slowly, everyone turned to look at Poppy. Her face flushed a little as she took out her wand. "Guess that'll be me," she smiled, shyly.

"Just wave your wand over the sword and the scrolls," Pickerel said. "Your kindness and the power of the Heart spark will do the rest."

Poppy glanced around her before she raised her wand high in the air. Then, she began to wave it above the scrolls, as though she were stirring a huge cauldron. To her amazement, the sword started to shine, then beautiful engravings appeared along the length of its shining blade.

Everyone gasped as the words on the leaf scrolls began to glow and lift off the page, just as the engravings on the sword came to life and leapt into the air, too. As they mixed with the words, everything transformed to create a moving picture, something like a movie showing on an invisible screen in midair.

"Is that Princess Sugarplum?" asked Holly in an astonished voice.

Pickerel nodded. But Princess Sugarplum didn't look the same as anyone had ever seen her before. Here, she was flying with her arms outstretched, the sword gripped in one hand. Below her were a group of boggarts, similar-looking to Pickerel but a little older. Princess Sugarplum looked fierce and determined—and although she was wearing a pink, frilly skirt, she also had on a sturdy chain mail vest.

"I *love* that chain mail!" said Ivy. "This is my kind of fairy princess!"

The friends watched in stunned silence as the scene changed to a battlefield—with Princess Sugarplum right in the middle of it! She wasn't hiding from the dragon toad, as the storybooks said. She was fighting it herself, with the boggarts helping her. Everyone cheered as the defeated dragon toad vanished with a pop.

"It always does that," said Azalea, airily.

"Wait a minute," said Holly, looking closely at the scene. "Who is *that*?" She pointed to a terrified-looking sprite quivering in the corner.

"That would be the, ahem, brave Prince Noble," Pickerel giggled. "The truth is that he set off to steal the dragon toad's treasure—but ended up being held captive by the toad instead. Prince Noble's family asked Princess Sugarplum for help, and she agreed without a second's thought. Once she had saved our not-so-heroic prince, she brought him back to Oakleaf Castle for a celebratory feast."

"Oakleaf Castle?" said Ivy.

"Oh, yes, of course!" said Poppy. "The Academy used to be a castle years ago. It's in one of my dad's books."

"That's right, it was Princess Sugarplum's castle. That's why the sword was hidden here," Pickerel explained.

As Poppy continued to wave her wand over the scene, the images changed again. This time, everyone saw a great banquet being held in the castle's grand hall. An important-looking boggart held out the pink-handled sword toward Princess Sugarplum, now engraved with pictures of her daring rescue.

As the feast continued, the fairies and boggarts ate and danced happily together. But then, the friends were shocked to see Prince Noble sneak over to Princess Sugarplum's chair and steal the sword!

Just then, the images began to fade,

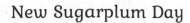

and Poppy lowered her wand. "What happened next?" Jessamy asked. "Are there any more scrolls Poppy can do her amazing swirly wand trick on?"

"There are no more scrolls," said Pickerel, "but we boggarts know what happened. Prince Noble didn't want anyone to see the pictures on the sword and find out what happened. So, he hid the sword and sent Princess Sugarplum on a quest to look for it. With her out of the way, he told everyone who would listen it was *he* who rescued Princess Sugarplum."

"Why didn't the boggarts tell everyone the truth?" asked Ivy.

"Well," said Pickerel, "Prince Noble soon became a king ... and *King* Noble was a very good liar. He told everyone that boggarts were dangerous tricksters. We've always kept to ourselves, and we live in dark, damp places. So it was

easy for people to imagine that we were secretive and sinister."

"I'm so sorry, Pickerel," said Ivy.

"It's not your fault," said Pickerel with a small smile. "You were told one version of the Princess Sugarplum story, and boggarts were told a different one."

"But your story is the truthful one," said Holly, sadly.

"It wasn't until I heard that a student at Oakleaf had been given the Heart spark that I started to hope the truth might finally come out," said Pickerel. "All I needed was to find the sword and the map that would show me where Prince Noble had hidden it. I just didn't realize that he'd given it to the dragon toad!"

"Well, the truth's definitely out now," said Poppy, happily. "We just need to make sure everyone hears the real story."

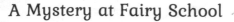

Holly looked at Ivy. The sisters grinned at each other. "Are you thinking what I'm thinking?" Holly asked.

Ivy nodded. "Come on, we have a lot of work to do!"

At last, it was Sugarplum Day! The day after they'd found out the truth about Princess Sugarplum, Holly and Ivy had written a whole new show for it. Ivy was going to play Princess Sugarplum herself, and she was excited to play the part of a daring, heroic fairy princess!

Ms. Peaseblossom had been shocked to hear the truth about Princess Sugarplum, but after Pickerel and Poppy had shown her the sword's magical engravings, she believed every word.

"Everyone ready?" asked Ms. Marigold,

as she looped her own guitar over her shoulder. Ivy nodded. Not only did she get to be Princess Sugarplum—she was also going to perform the opening song to the show with Interstella! She and Holly had written it together, and Ms. Marigold had said it was so good, they should think about starting a band together!

"Only after you've done all your homework, Ivy," Holly had teased.

Ms. Peaseblossom announced the

start of the show, then Holly, Ivy, and Ms. Marigold began their song, which was about boggarts and fairies becoming friends. Ivy couldn't help smiling at all the shocked faces in the crowd.

At the end of the song, Ivy hurried off the stage to grab the rest of her props and returned ready to play the magical princess. Dandelion, the pixie from Ivy's Ariel class, played Prince Noble, and

Olive and Oakley, the gnome twins, lit up the stage with their glittering jewels. Even Pickerel appeared, playing the boggart who gave Princess Sugarplum her magical sword at the feast.

The crowd cheered at brave Princess Sugarplum and booed at the cowardly Prince Noble. When the curtain came down at the end of the show, loud applause echoed around the hall.

"Very well done, everyone!" Ms. Peaseblossom said, clapping the performers backstage. She fluttered over to Ivy and smiled. "See, didn't I say you would have fun on Sugarplum Day?"

Ivy laughed as Ms. Marigold fluttered over to join them. "Never mind my sister," she said, rolling her eyes. "She always had to be right when we were growing up, too!"

"You're so different for sisters," Ivy said. "Just like us. Holly's so, well, fairylike, and I'm so ... not. Have you always been friends, though?"

Ms. Peaseblossom laughed. "We've certainly had our arguments! But we always make up. You see, there's no right or wrong way of being a fairy. And that goes for being a sister, too!"